THE
KILLER CAT
RUNS AWAY

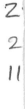

www.randomhousechildrens.co.uk

ANNE FINE

THE KILLER CAT RUNS AWAY

Illustrated by Thomas Docherty

CORGI YEARLING

THE KILLER CAT RUNS AWAY
A CORGI YEARLING BOOK 978 0 440 87011 1

First published in Great Britain by Doubleday,
an imprint of of Random House Children's Publishers UK
A Random House Group Company

Hardback edition published 2013
This edition published 2014

1 3 5 7 9 10 8 6 4 2

The Random House Group Limited supports the Forest Stewardship Council®
(FSC®), the leading international forest-certification organisation. Our
books carrying the FSC label are printed on FSC®-certified paper. FSC is the only
forest-certification scheme supported by the leading environmental organisations,
including Greenpeace. Our paper procurement policy can be found at
www.randomhouse.co.uk/environment.

MIX
Paper from
responsible sources
FSC® C016897

Set in Palatino

Corgi Yearling Books are published by Random House Children's Publishers UK,
61-63 Uxbridge Road, London, W5 5SA

www.randomhousechildrens.co.uk
www.totallyrandombooks.co.uk
www.randomhouse.co.uk

Addresses for companies within The Random House Group Limited can be
found at: www.randomhouse.co.uk/offices.htm

THE RANDOM HOUSE GROUP Limited Reg. No. 954009

A CIP catalogue record for this book is available from the British Library.

Printed and bound in Great Britain by CPI Group (UK) Ltd, Croydon, CR0 4YY

CONTENTS

1

Silly Pink Babies

OK, OK. So twist my tail. I spat at the stupid
baby. But it was *annoying* me, lying there in its
frilly basket, chuckling and gurgling. The thing
was *laughing* at me. And no one likes being
laughed at. Especially not me. I'm not called
Tuffy for nothing. And I didn't earn the nick-
name of 'the killer cat' from sitting purring on
a cushion.

And then this baby poked its finger in my
eye. For heaven's sake! It could have hurt me.
So it was lucky, really. I could have bitten it. Or
scratched it. But I only spat. Spit doesn't hurt at
all, so why's everyone picking on me?

'Tuffy!' said Ellie. 'Get away from the baby at once!'

She rushed to scoop it up. I don't know why. It wasn't even yelling. The baby didn't mind. It was still laughing as if the whole thing was a giant joke. And there was only a tiny bit of dribble running down its face. Nobody in this house has any sense of humour at all. They all go mad about the slightest thing.

'That cat is not to be trusted,' said Ellie's father. 'He's the most jealous creature under the sun.'

I like that! Jealous? Me? Of something that can't even walk or feed itself? I gave the man the slit-eyed stare. But he just stared right back and said to Ellie, 'Remember poor Tinkerbell?'

Ellie went pale. Of course she remembered. Tinkerbell was a small kitten the family had to look after for four whole days. You wouldn't believe the fuss they made of her.

'Isn't she pretty? So fluffy! And so sweet!'

'Look, Ellie! Tinkerbell's learned how to flick her tail!'

'See her tiny pink tongue! Look, Mum! Look quickly, while she's lapping up her milk!'

'She's not cold, is she? If she's cold, push Tuffy off the rug and let Tinkerbell sit near the fire instead.'

'I think she's hungry. Shall we offer her a dish of cream?'

Offer her cream? She didn't even live with us! We were just kitten-sitting for a day or so.

And I was their real pet, not Tinkerbell. I'd lived with them for years, ever since Ellie got old enough to nag them into getting me. Is it surprising that I got a little testy?

And that I wouldn't let Tinkerbell sleep in any of my favourite places.

And that I accidentally pushed her off the windowsill.

And ate her special, juicy baby kitten food, all by mistake.

And all the other stupid, petty things that they complained about. No, I don't think that Tinkerbell will be in any hurry to come and stay with us again.

And there's no room, in any case. Because they clearly prefer silly pink babies now.

If they're not careful I shall spit at it again.

2

Parasite

OK, OK. So cover me with jam and put me in a box of wasps. I broke their new television. It was an *accident*! I didn't mean to tip the screen over like that. I was after a bumblebee, and if that stupid television hadn't been in the way, I would have got it too. No one likes being stung by bees. They should have been *grateful* to me.

And whose fault was it that the new, slim, wide, high-definition screen wasn't fixed on its stand more safely in the first place?

Yes! That's right. It was Ellie's dad's fault, not mine. You only had to watch Mr Oh-That'll-Probably-Be-All-Right fixing the screen so loosely onto the base to know that it was almost bound to fall off. Even without someone like me crashing into it hard.

And whose fault was it that I didn't manage to get over the screen in my amazing leap?

That's right. It was Ellie's *mother's* fault. She is the one who feeds me. If she has got it wrong and let me get a smidgeon over my ideal jumping weight, who is to blame?

Clearly not me.

You should have heard Ellie's dad when he came in and saw the damage. Talk about wild!

'This screen is ruined! Ruined! Claw marks all over, and both the top corners chipped! Look what that great, fat, stupid, tiresome, idiotic, unpleasant, vicious, dangerous parasite has done now!'

Excuse me? *Parasite?*

Now that's not nice. In case you don't already know, parasites are all those nasty things like nits and tapeworms and fleas and ticks that do nothing except sponge off other people to stay alive. I am not like that. I let myself be stroked. I let myself be fed. I let myself be cuddled. (Only by Ellie. And only *sometimes*. But you take my point.)

I'm not a parasite. How *dare* he? I won't put up with rudeness like that. I tell you, next time he looks in his chest of drawers, he's going to find hairs over everything. On all his socks. And on his pants and vests. Don't think I can't lick quite enough hairs off me to make his underwear *disgusting*.

I can pay him back.

3

The Same Old Boring Cat-Chat

He was a whole lot crosser than I thought.
I slipped out for a quick smell tour around
the wheelie bins with Tiger and Bella and
Snowball. But when I strolled back in, what
should I come across but what he calls 'a family
conference' and I call 'The Same Old Boring Cat-
Chat that I've heard over a thousand times'.

'What shall we do about Tuffy?'

There they all were, huddled together in
the living room: Old Mr Grumpy. The Kitten-
Loving Queen. And Ellie.

I hung around outside the door, eaves-
dropping as usual.

'So,' says Mr Football-on-Telly-Addict-Gone-Mad, 'I say that was the last straw, and we should find another home for Tuffy.'

Just like she always does, Ellie burst into tears. 'No! No! You can't! Tuffy's my pet!'

Her mother usually sticks up for me. But not this time. 'But he's not safe with babies. Or with kittens.'

'Or televisions,' Ellie's dad added bitterly, still harping on about his own sad loss.

Now Ellie stamped her foot. 'But he's my *pet*!'

That's when her father turned even more cunning than usual. 'Ellie, I know you're very fond of Tuffy. But we could always find you another pet.'

'Yes,' said her mother. 'One that's a bit more gentle and doesn't cause quite so much damage.'

'Perhaps a kitten . . .' said her dad.

'Like Tinkerbell . . .' her mother said hopefully.

'But what about *Tuffy*?' Ellie said through her tears. 'What will happen to him?'

'Oh, you know cats,' said Mr Get-What-You-Want-Whichever-Sneaky-Way-You-Can. 'They're not like dogs. They don't *adore* their owners. So long as they're warm and comfy, and the grub's good, cats can be happy anywhere. And there are plenty of other places Tuffy could go.'

I took a peek round the door and saw Ellie's mother shaking her head at the pulled threads on her sofa where I like to scratch to keep my claws in trim. 'Yes,' she agreed. 'Homes that are far more suitable than ours.'

'That's right,' said Ellie's father. 'We'll find a home where he'll be just as happy.'

This is the moment when Ellie always hurls herself face down on the sofa, sobbing and wailing, and threatens to run away if they get rid of me, her precious pet. This is the moment when she's supposed to shout at them: 'If you don't love dear Tuffy enough to keep him, then you don't love me!'

But there was silence.

Just a long, long silence.

The longest silence *ever*.

I peered round the door again and couldn't believe my eyes! Ellie was dashing away her tears and looking hopeful.

'Really? Another home where Tuffy will be just as happy?'

'That's right!' said Mr I-Never-Did-Like-That-Cat-Anyway.

'And I could have another pet? A pretty kitten, just like Tinkerbell?'

'Why not?'

Shall I tell you what I did then? I sat behind the door and waited. And I didn't just wait.

I *counted* to myself. One, two, three, four . . .

And would you like to know how long it took before Ellie burst into tears again and started sticking up for me?

It took eleven seconds! Can you believe it? Eleven whole seconds before that disloyal child finally remembered who is supposed to be her amazing, precious Tuffy. The Tuffy she even thinks she will be taking to the special 'My Wonderful Pet' show in her school hall next Thursday evening. (Ho, ho! She'll be lucky!) The Tuffy she loves 'so much and always have and always will, for ever and ever and ever'.

Eleven great long seconds!

What a cheek!

4

One Good Reason to Stay

That night I told the gang, 'I'm going to run away.'

They all stared. 'Run away? But *why*?'

'Because I'm not happy at home.'

'What's wrong with your home?' demanded Tiger. 'The place is warm, isn't it?'

'Well, yes,' I had to admit. 'The place is warm.'

'And comfy enough,' said Bella.

'Yes, I grant you it's comfy enough,' I said reluctantly.

Snowball said, 'And the grub in your house is very good indeed.'

'Obviously the grub is good,' I said, 'or

I wouldn't still be there.' I waved an irritable paw. 'But give me one good reason why I ought to stay.'

'Apart from the fact that it's warm, and comfy, and the grub is good?'

'Yes,' I said. 'Apart from that.'

They all had a good long think. But none of them could come up with a single reason why I ought to stay (apart from the fact that the house is warm and comfy, and the grub is good).

'Well, there you go,' I said triumphantly when they had racked their brains. 'Not one of you can think of anything. So I have no choice but to run away.'

5

A Chapter of Sad Farewells

I went around saying fond farewells to all the things I've loved so long.

'Goodbye, dear Pot Plant,' I said. 'I expect that you'll miss me scratching around in your soil when it's too cold and wet for me to bother to go outside to do my business.' I brushed away a tear. 'And I shall miss you too.'

I went into the kitchen.

'*Adieu*, my beloved Frying Pan,' I sighed. 'How many times have I stood beside you on the counter, licking your leftover bacon fat when no one else was about! We have been friends for so long, Frying Pan. But this is the end.'

I went upstairs.

'This is the parting of the ways,' I told Alarm Clock. 'But we have shared so many happy moments. How often I have crept in here by moonlight when Mr I-Must-Not-Be-Late has set you carefully for seven o'clock. How often I have braved his rattling snores to jump on the bedside table and reach out a silent paw to push your ON button to OFF. And how the two of us have enjoyed his desperate shrieks of panic when he wakes late in the morning. Oh, I shall miss you, Alarm Clock!'

I slid under Mr I-Do-*Not*-Snore-I-Just-Breathe-Heavily's side of the bed.

'So long, Bedroom Slippers,' I said. 'If I had a single tear for every dead mouse I've slipped into your toes to frighten Mr Oh-My-Lord-What's-*This*?, then I could weep a river to say goodbye to you. Please don't feel lonely and neglected without my little gifts. Goodbye! Goodbye!'

I went downstairs to the piano.

'*Adios*, my musical friend! After today I shall walk up and down your keys no more, making you plink and plunk and driving everyone mad. Our happy hours are over. I'm off into the world, and we shall sadly never finish our masterwork: *The Tuffy Piano Concerto for Four Paws*.'

I thought it would be nice to leave with that sweet tune still ringing in my ears. So I walked up and down the keys a bit. (I like to stick to the black ones. They sound more plinky-plunky. And every time one of my paws slides off onto a white key, I tend to get a little cross, and stamp.)

'What is that *dreadful* noise?'

Whoops! Mr Not-At-All-Musical poked his head round the door. 'You! Well, you can get off that piano at once!'

He pushed me off. I *hate* that, so I spun round in the air on my way down and scratched him hard.

'Yeee-*ouch*!'

He glared at me, and I glared back at him.

That is one person in this house to whom I won't be saying any fond farewell.

6

So Spank My Bum

So spank my furry little bum, I didn't say goodbye to Ellie. I meant to. That's why I went back up the stairs and into her bedroom. That's why I jumped up at her side and started to purr in her ear.

Then I saw what she was looking at on her computer screen.

Kittens!

Cute baby fluff-balls. Sweet little winsome things with huge eyes staring out. You wouldn't believe their names. Sugar-Pie. Binty-Minty. Pansy-Wansy. Prissy-Missy. (Excuse me while I stick a paw down my throat.)

Ellie stopped at the photo of a kitten called Titania. (I ask you! Titania! For a *cat*!)

'Look, Tuffy. Isn't she *cute*?'

Sometimes I think it's a good thing that I can't speak. Because if I could, I would have told young Ellie just what I think of idiotic, brainless balls of fluff that can't clean their own fur or creep up on anything taking a quick nap in a nest. Why, some of them can't even find the way to the litter tray on their tenth day.

So it's a good job I don't talk. I wouldn't have liked the last few words that I exchanged with Ellie to be unpleasant.

So I never said goodbye.

7

Dead Mice and Birds?
Eee-*yuk!*

Out on the wall, the gang were waiting.

'So,' Bella said. 'You're really off?'

'Yes,' I said proudly. 'I'm not going to stay where I'm not wanted.'

They were still anxious. 'But, Tuffy, if no one in Ellie's family is there to put your food in front of you, what are you going to *eat*?'

I had a think. In the end I said, 'I am a cat, so if I don't find anything else, there's always the old traditional stand-by.'

They all looked blank.

'Dead mice and birds,' I said.

I don't think I have ever seen three faces look more disgusted.

'Dead mice and birds? Eee-*yuk*!'

'You're joking!'

'What, pick off all that hair and fur and feathers and stuff, and actually *eat* the things?'

'Revolting!'

'Horror-show idea!'

'Full gross-out!'

'What a sick plan! You must be off your head.'

'Listen,' I said. 'Dead mice and birds is what cats *used* to eat.'

They weren't convinced. 'Yes. Back in the *Stone* Age!'

'Before cat food was invented.'

'About a million years ago.'

'Don't be such wimps,' I told them. 'Why, I can remember my mother telling me proudly that my own great-grandfather was known as a splendid mouser.'

'I bet he didn't *eat* the things he caught.'

'I bet he did,' I argued.

Tiger was determined. 'No way. He'd have been sick.'

'I'd have been sick just *watching* him,' added Snowball.

I wasn't going to hang around and argue. It was getting dark. So I got Bella and Snowball to hold my collar tight while I slipped out of it.

Then, 'Farewell, gang!' I said. 'I'm off to seek my fortune. Wish me luck!'

They all came further along the wall to watch me go. Tiger waved a forlorn paw. 'Don't you forget us, Tuffy!'

'No, don't forget us. We won't ever forget you.'

'No, never.'

8

Tuffy the Busker

I thought it best to go where no one knew me. After all, I didn't want nosy people peering down at me. 'Aren't you that cat from Acacia Avenue that dug up all my petunias? I'm going to take you home.'

So I went further into town than I do usually. It was quite busy. There were a lot of people standing at bus stops and hurrying across the streets. I wandered up and down till, from round the corner, I heard someone playing a tune I like on a mouth organ.

I stopped to listen. Whoever was playing began to sing the words:

'Scooby-scooby, swish-swish
Fishy in a dish-dish
Make a little wish-wish
That it tastes delish-lish.'

Just the thought made me feel peckish. I turned the corner, and there in a doorway stood a young man. He'd put a paper plate on the pavement, and passers-by were putting down their shopping bags and fishing in their pockets to toss in coins.

A busker!

He had been given quite a lot of money. I watched for a while, and every few minutes he'd scoop up a few coins and put them in his pocket. Then he'd start singing again.

I could do that! I could sing too, and maybe some of the shoppers would open their bags and drop me a tiny chunk of chicken from their ready-cooked suppers, or peel a slice of smoked salmon off the top of their pack.

Yum, yum. Delish-lish!

So I went round the next corner to find a doorway for myself, and to collect the little gifts that I expected to get I dragged a fairly clean takeaway dinner tray out of the gutter.

And then I sang.

I sang my little heart out. First I tried charming them with that forlorn old song about the kitten whose paws get frozen in the snow.

Then I sang that song that makes soft people weep about the tabby cat who starves to death up a tree. (Per-*lease*! How old are *you*? And how many cats' skeletons have you seen dangling from high branches so far in life? None. That's right. *None*.)

And then I gave my all to my own favourite, *The Wild Cats' Chorus*.

None of them worked. Not one. People just clutched their heads and hurried by. Some of them even glowered. Nobody bothered to stop to say, 'What charming melodies! And what a lovely voice!'

In fact, they were quite rude. I kept hearing snatches of what they said as they rushed past.

'. . . horrible yowling noise . . .'

'. . . shouldn't be allowed . . .'

'. . . perfectly *ghastly* . . .'

'. . . clearly in *misery*. Ought to be put down . . .'

Then one man had the cheek to pick up my collection tray and drop it in the litter bin along the street.

I gave up singing then, and just walked on. Time for another plan.

9

The Wild Cats' Chorus

This time I was smart. I walked up a nice-looking road and found a nice-looking house with a nice-looking lady unloading nice-looking groceries from her nice-looking car.

She looked a tiny bit familiar. But then, I get about. I've met a lot of people. So anyhow, I thought, This place will do.

First thing: get introduced. I wrapped myself round her legs, all the time purring madly.

The woman reached down to stroke me. Suddenly she looked a little nervous. 'Hang on,' she said. 'Haven't I seen you before? Wasn't it you who got in a flying fur fight with another cat in our school playground once, and upset all my tiny Year Ones?'

Uh-oh! Now I remembered who she was! Ellie's head teacher!

But I was hungry, and they were nice-looking groceries. So I turned the purring up to Regulo 8. It worked a treat. 'Oh, no,' she said. 'I must be wrong. You're such a sweet and friendly cat, and that one was downright *horrible*. Why, our school crossing guard still has a scar where that vile animal scratched her.'

I tried to look sympathetic as I followed her inside the house. I kept up the heavy purring while she put away her shopping. Then she bent down to feel around my neck.

'No collar.'

Of course, no collar. I am a good deal smarter than that!

She sighed. 'Oh, dear. I suppose I'd better feed you.' She shook a finger. 'But it's just this once!'

Just this once? Ho, ho, ho. Everyone knows if you feed a cat once, it has you on a string for life. So I was in. She fed me tuna from a can, and picked me up to carry me around. I didn't struggle at all. It was an act of will, but I kept purring.

Even when she showed me her parrot.

'Look,' she said, pointing to his cage. 'Meet Gregory.'

Gregory the Parrot gave me the blink, and I blinked back.

'I hope you'll both be friends,' she said.

I purred my hardest.

'Gregory's very clever,' she told me. 'I'm going to shut you in the kitchen. But if you hear lots of odd noises and voices while I'm out, you mustn't be afraid. That'll be Gregory imitating things he's heard.'

I purred and nodded.

'Good,' she said. 'Now I'm afraid I have to nip back to school to sort out a few things for the special "My Wonderful Pet" show we're holding on Thursday evening. I'll find your owner to-morrow. But just for tonight, you can stay here.'

She picked up her briefcase and left.

So I sat in the kitchen.

Just a kitchen.

Boring. Dead boring.

Then Gregory started up. First he did 'creaking door' and 'the wheelie-bin rumble'. After that he did 'Fireworks Night'. Then he did his owner saying, 'Oh, Gregory! You know I get headaches from horrid noises. Can't you do something quiet and *nice*?'

OK, OK. So boil me in bunny juice! I taught him *The Wild Cats' Chorus*. I yowled it from the kitchen, and Gregory the Parrot picked it up in no time. Soon we were yowling away together

so it was twice as loud, and he learned how to do that too. And by the time I'd had enough of singing along with him, Gregory could sound like four cats singing, not just one, all by himself.

Stellar!

The problem was that he was so excited with his new trick he kept it up for two whole hours after Ellie's head teacher came back.

So naturally I got thrown out.

10

The Perfect Home

I spent the night in the tool shed. Then, in the morning, I set off to find a better home. I had a tiny thought that I might go back to Ellie. I was quite sure she would have realized her mistake by now, and be lying face down on her bed, sobbing her poor broken heart out and wailing my name to the heavens.

But as I strolled along the street, what should I see but a notice stuck on a lamppost.

And then another.

And another.

And more and more. All the same.

I stretched up to take a look. It was a 'lost

cat' notice, with a photo of the roughest, toughest, sourest, grumpiest-looking moggie you've ever seen in your life.

I couldn't help but think: Who'd want to have *that* thug back?

Then I peered a little closer.

It was *me*.

I took a long look down the street. Sure enough, far in the distance I could see Ellie's mum, stopping at every lamppost to stick up yet another of her insulting posters.

The *cheek* of it! For one thing, I am not a 'lost cat'. I am a cat who has moved on to better things! And for another, they'd picked the worst photo ever. *Not* my best side. I mean, I do not look like that! Not all the time, anyhow! Not every day. Sometimes – perhaps – if I am in a really fed-up mood. But hardly ever! Almost never!

No one would recognize me from that photo. No one. Not in a million years!

So I strolled on quite happily – though it was odd how many people I saw glance at the posters then bend down to try to pick me up. (I simply spat them off.)

And then I found what I was looking for.

The perfect home.

It had wide windowsills to lounge on. The garden was a jungle. (Good hunting there!) Some of the windows were unlatched. The wheelie-bin lid was off. And, best of all, there was a fish pond with sweet little goldfish dart-ing about in it.

Oh, bliss! Oh, sheer and perfect bliss! If there's one thing I love to do, it's stretch out along the side of a fish pond in the sun and idly dip in a paw to try to—

No. No time to think about that now! I went to meet the owner. He was washing up. We had a conversation. It went like this:

Him: *Hello, puss. Where did you spring from?*

Me: *Purr, purr.* (I'm slinking round his legs to let him know I'm feeling peckish.)

Him: *Hungry? Fancy some leftover fish?*

Me: *Purrrrrrrrrrr!*

Him (putting down a dish): *There you go. Finish that lot and you'll feel a whole lot better.*

Me: *Chomp, chomp, chomp.*

I thought I was in heaven. I ate the fish. (A little too much dill, I thought. But, hey! not everyone's a master chef.) I had a nap on one of his windowsills. When it got chilly I slipped back into the house through one of the un-latched windows, and when I felt like a snack at lunch time, I set off for the little pond.

Shame! He was out there, hanging out the washing.

Well, never mind. Fish fresh as that will keep. I took a turn round the side of the house and had a poke through the recycling bins.

Half a fish finger. Delish-lish. Just like the

song. Yes, I'd found The Perfect Home.

Or so I thought. But then, at half-past three, my world caved in. There was a stampede up the garden path. A pack of carrot-topped hooligans, all shrieking and yelling.

'Look! On the windowsill! A cat!'

'Daddy's got us a real pet! Not just those stupid goldfish, but a real live cat!'

'Bagsy I cuddle it first.'

'No! I'm the one who saw it, so I get first cuddle.'

'Then me.'

'Then me.'

'Then me!'

'Well, if I'm last, I want to be the one to take it in to school for the "My Wonderful Pet" show!'

Nice to be wanted, of course. But really, the noise was horrendous! While they were crowding round, I counted them. Five carrot-tops! Five horrid noisy children all reaching out to grab me. I tell you, it took a good bit of hissing and spitting to get off that windowsill.

Didn't they change their tune then!

'The horrid thing!'

'It's scratched me! Look! I'm actually *bleeding*!'

'It must be *wild*.'

'Who'd want to take *that* into school? I'd rather show everyone our lovely goldfish.'

'We didn't really want a new pet anyway.'

'Well, we certainly didn't want *this* one.'

A good thing too, because I wasn't staying. The Perfect Home, indeed! I don't think so.

11

'Come Home So I Can Strangle You.'

I took a nap in next door's garage. (OK, OK! So twist my tail! I left a dent in the fancy new hat some man was hiding in there till his wife's birthday. But anybody napping in there would have used it as a little bed. That hat was *comfy*. It wasn't *my* fault that the ribbon round the brim got tangled and torn. All I was trying to do was brush off the cat hairs that I shed on it while I was having my snooze.)

I woke up *starving*. Back at my old house, when I was hungry I simply parked myself on my big furry bottom somewhere really inconvenient and *stared* at Ellie's mum till she remembered to feed me.

Sadly, that does not work with strangers who are hurrying by. I had to keep stepping in their path and wrapping myself round their ankles (the way I used to do with Ellie when I was getting bored).

But strangers are so *clumsy*. I got tripped over and stumbled into several times. And snarled at quite a lot. Some people were quite *rude*. In the end I gave up and went to check what had been thrown out by the nearest pizza place. (Don't you *adore* pepperoni?)

Just as I came round the corner, who should I see stamping past in a tantrum but Mr I've-Been-Sent-Out-To-Look-For-Our-Cat.

I didn't fancy being carried back by him, so I slunk out of sight.

'Puss, puss!' I heard him calling to the wind. 'Tuff! Tuff-eee! Where *are* you? Come home so I can strangle you! Come home so I can boil you in oil! Tuff-eee! Do you know what's on telly at this very moment? Yes! The Best-Ever Penalty Shoot-out Show! And am I sitting watching it? No, I am not! Partly because the television is *ruined*. And partly because I've been sent out to find you! So come home, Tuffy! Puss, puss, puss! Come home so I can spoil your life the same way that you spoil mine!'

I ask a simple question. If you heard that, would *you* be stupid enough to pad out from the shadows and show yourself?

No, you would not.

I wouldn't, either. All thoughts of going home had vanished once again, so I turned round and slunk off fast the other way.

12

I Did Not Kill It!

(Here is a warning. Those of you who are 'of a nervous disposition' – and that means wet – had better skip this chapter. It isn't nice.)

I tramped the streets. The hours went by. And I got hungrier.

And hungrier.

And hungrier.

Everyone's wheelie bin lids were fixed on tight. I went through one garden after another on the prowl, hoping that someone had at least put out a dish of milk for a hedgehog to keep me going.

But there was nothing.

I made my way right to the end of a row of gardens.

Nothing.

Sighing, I made my way back again. That's when I saw it lying on the grass under my feet.

A baby bird.

I did not kill it! Understand? It must have fallen out of its nest after I went by the first time. (Possibly from fright.)

But it was dead. (And fresh.)

And I was hungry.

I gave the thing a little poke. 'Come on!' I told myself. 'Don't be so *mimsy*! It's meat. It's fresh. It's nice and traditional. And you are very hungry.'

Alas! Nowhere *near* hungry enough, my friend. Nowhere *near* hungry enough.

Bella and Tiger and Snowball were right.

Eeee-*yuk*!!!

13

' A Photo of My Beautiful Tuffy!'

So there I was, still trying to persuade myself that baby bird would taste as good as pepperoni, when a shadow fell over me.

A woman had come out of the house.

I stared at her. She stared at me. I stared at her because she'd done her hair so that it looked like one of those whippy ice-cream cones.

She stared at me as though she thought I were a gift from heaven.

'A cat!' She looked at the sad little mess between my paws. 'And clearly a hunter! Are you a mouser too? Because there's a rustling somewhere near my kitchen door. I think I might have *vermin*!'

You could tell she was fussy just from the way she said *'vermin!'*. But I was tired and hungry, so I thought – why not? Some cats do earn their keep. I could give it a go.

And I was right to try. Because life there could have been perfect bliss! Ms Whippy thought that she was keeping me hungry enough to eat mice, but what she didn't know is that I'm good with kitchen bins. Every time she went out, I'd step on the pedal, and when the lid flew up I'd reach inside to hook out some half-eaten chop, or the last of the chicken. After I'd had enough, I'd carry the leftovers out into the garden and kick them out of sight behind her precious lupins.

She didn't get suspicious because the

rustling stopped. (It only came from some dried leaf trapped under the kitchen door. I poked that out and – hey, presto! – all the vermin gone.)

For three nights in a row, she sang my praises. 'You're brilliant, Pusskins. I could do with a mouser like you in my villa in Spain.'

Her villa in Spain? Was she a *millionaire*?

You'd think so. First she bought me a fancy jewelled collar and a swansdown cat bed. (Purrrrr!) Then she bought me a classy water bowl. On the next day she even took me into town to have my photo taken. Yes! None of that cheap, 'Hold still while I fetch my mobile!' stuff that I'd been used to back in Ellie's house. Ms Whippy took me into town to get a proper studio portrait! The photographer sat me on a cushion and asked me most politely to face the camera. 'Pusskins! Please look this way! Yes! That's much better.'

A dozen different shots were taken, and I must say they came out very nicely indeed.

(Much better than those horrid 'lost cat' posters.) I was so pleased I thought I'd take one round to show my old ungrateful family what they were missing. I picked one up by the corner and (trying not to drool) carried it carefully across town to my old home.

Ellie was sitting on the doorstep, weeping bitterly.

I shot behind a bush.

'Oh, Tuffy!' she was whimpering. 'Oh, Tuffy! You've been away so long! And how I miss you! Oh, Tuffy, I wish you'd come home!'

Home? Ha! Excuse me, but I have a new home now. A much, much better home where I dine on the finest foods, and people truly know how beautiful I am.

I spat the photograph out of my mouth and watched it slither in the breeze up the path towards Ellie.

Curious, she picked it up, dashing away her tears so she could peer at it more closely. Then she began to wail. 'Oh, no! A photo of my beautiful Tuffy! And it's not one I've ever seen before!'

Too true, it wasn't. It was far smarter and glossier than any photo they'd ever had of me.

Ellie rushed into the house. I jumped up out of sight behind the laurel bush and peered in through the window. Ellie was waving the photo in her parents' faces. 'Mum! Dad! Look!

Tuffy must have been catnapped! See? The catnappers have sent a photograph to prove it.'

I will admit that Ellie's mum looked most concerned. But Mr Don't-Expect-Me-To-Put-*My*-Hand-In-My-Pocket just muttered something most unpleasant along the lines of, 'If that pesky cat's worth even a handful of loose change, I'm a banana.' If I'd not been in hiding, I'd have spat at him. Right in the face.

Ellie burst into tears again, and I jumped down. Don't you feel sorry for Ellie! Don't you dare! It's her own fault! She should have thought about how much she would miss her precious Tuffy before she started mooning over soppy kittens on the computer screen.

So don't you get your knickers in a twist worrying about Ellie.

You worry about *me*.

That's what *I* did. I suddenly thought, If I don't get back quickly, fussy Ms Whippy will have emptied the pedal bin before I've had time to rescue my supper.

So I hurried off.

14

Nightmare Stuff!

Ms Whippy talked a lot on the phone to her friends about her villa in Spain. It sounded *horrible*. I'd find the weather far too hot, I am not overly fond of garlic, and I hate walking on tiles because they make my claws click.

Also, why would I care about her lovely private pool? I'm not a swimming cat. No, every time I heard her talk about that villa of hers, I shuddered quietly and thought how glad I was that I live here.

That's why finding the papers was such a shock.

I wasn't *snooping*. It's just a well-known fact that, if there is a bit of paper lying on a table, that's what a cat will sit on.

Even if it's as small as a bus ticket, that's where we'll sit.

And this paper was full-size. I sat on it for quite a while. (OK, OK! So dip my paws in soap suds! I had been trying to spread the leftovers of my supper out a little bit behind her lupins and my paws were still chickeny. I made a mess.)

That's why I glanced down at the paper I was sitting on – to see if there were any more tiny scraps of chicken that had dried enough to be flicked onto the floor.

That's when I saw the word PASSPORT.

I looked a little closer and saw PET.

I lifted my bum and stepped back so that I could read the whole thing. TWENTY-FOUR-HOUR PET PASSPORT APPLICATION.

Aha! The truth was out! Ms Whippy hadn't taken me to get a photo simply because of my good looks. She wanted it for a passport so she could take me to her villa in Spain to be a mouser there!

I read the small print. It was nightmare stuff! First, there was a rule about carrying a letter from the vet that proved your pet was up-to-date with injections. (Injections! In case you live on Mars, I'll have you know that that means needles. Not my favourite things. And vets! Not my favourite people.)

Then came a rule about the size of the wire cage. 'Cage', you notice. Not 'comfy basket' or 'cosy box'. Wire cage!

There was a bit about how long your pet would spend in the baggage hold. The baggage hold! Like some old suitcase!

There was a rule about the photo of your pet having to be full-face.

A full-face photograph? Well, didn't all that sweet-talking, 'Pusskins, please look this way. Yes, that's much better,' sound a bit different now!

And then I read the last line, just above Ms Whippy's flowery signature.

The date of travel.

5th May, she'd written.

5th May? I looked up at the calendar.

It was the 4th!

15

A Blur of Fur

Ever seen a tornado?

Even if the answer's yes, you've not seen anything as fast as me getting out of that house. I was a *rocket*. I was a blur of fur that shot through that open window and up the garden path in less than half a blink. I moved so fast that I looked back to see myself pretty well still leaping out.

That was my big mistake. I should have kept my eyes ahead because, before I could even catch my breath, I felt myself being snatched up and heard a man's voice. 'Aha! Trying to make a getaway, are you, Pusskins? Well, tough luck! Gotcha!'

I swivelled my head round to look. Yee-ow! The man was dressed in one of those short white coats our vet wears at her surgery.

I wriggled frantically, but all he did was hold me even more tightly. 'Stop struggling, Pusskins! No point in my driving all the way here for a special home pick-up if my patient has fled.'

Patient? Victim, more like! I've had my shots already! I don't need any more. So I kept struggling madly. I scratched. I hissed. I yowled. I put up a tremendous fight. But this guy was clearly a master at hanging onto squirming animals. Before I even realized what was happening, he'd carried me round to Ms Whippy's suntrap patio, and used his teeth to pull a towel down from her rotary washing line to wrap me up in it.

Me! Held fast in a roll of fluffy pink! I looked like a struggling sausage.

Small wonder I hate vets. They'll get you every time. I bet they even take classes in rolling harmless little pussy cats up in old towels so they can shove pills down their throats and stick needles into them.

He carried me back to the front of the house and rang the bell. Ms Whippy must have torn herself away from packing all her fancy clothes because she came to the door.

My captor held me up. 'Your cat's a smart one. He was trying to get away.'

Ms Whippy clasped her hands under her

chin. 'Oh, no!' she said. 'Thank heavens you stopped him. If he doesn't have his shots we can't go, and the flight is tomorrow.'

'No problem,' smarmed our most un-welcome visitor. 'I'll have him back to you tonight with all the paperwork you need.'

I tried to tell them I had *had* my shots. All of them. Way back in March. But it came out as one enormous yowl.

And then a ghastly thing happened.

Ms Whippy leaned forward suddenly and kissed me on the nose.

Me! Tuffy! On the nose! A sloppy kiss!

Only one word for that. 'Yee-*uk*!'

16

Whistling cheerfully, the vet carried me back
down to his van and unfurled me out of the
fluffy pink towel into a cage. He dumped
the cage down on the passenger seat.

So boil me in bunny juice. I hissed and spat.

'Temper, temper,' he said reprovingly.

We drove a mile
or two and then
his mobile rang.
The vet pulled
off the road
and rang the
number back.

I only heard his side of the conversation. 'Hi, Arif. What's the problem?'

Arif must have explained because the next words were, 'You need a cat?'

Excuse me? Was he talking to a madman? Who on earth *needs* a cat? I mean, we don't do anything useful. We cost a lot to feed. We ruin the furniture. We do exactly what we want.

I ask the question again. Who *needs* a cat?

But clearly this Arif did, because when I tuned in again it was to hear the vet ringing Ms Whippy to check she didn't mind if he lent me to some other vet he knew. 'It's only for half an hour, and I must say your Pusskins would be perfect for the job.'

Hear that? 'Perfect'.

Obviously Ms Whippy agreed. So I admit that, by the time we met Arif somewhere around the park five minutes later, my head was already swelling.

'Watch him!' the vet warned as he handed my cage to Arif. 'He's in the foulest mood. But he's the only cat booked into the surgery this evening. I have to give him all his shots tonight, so he can fly to Spain tomorrow.'

'If the plane gets off the ground!'

I didn't get the joke, but they still shared a laugh and then the vet climbed back in his van. 'Be careful,' he warned Arif, just before driving off. 'That cat is *horribly* fierce so, whatever you do, don't let anyone open his cage!'

Oh, thanks a bunch! What happened to my being 'perfect', I wondered as we set off down the street. I can't say that Arif was the most considerate cat-cage carrier. He swung it till I was slipping from side to side like someone on board a ship in a gale. I paid him out by spitting through the bars and reaching out a paw to pull so many woollen threads out of his fancy jumper that I was practically hidden behind the tangles.

But my heart wasn't in it. I was *miserable*. You know me. I am not one to wallow in despair and live my life in fear of what might lie round the next corner. But I admit that I was feeling really *glum*. I had set off with such high hopes: a better life, a nicer home and more appreciative company. People who recognized my true worth. People who saw me for the handsome, valiant, resourceful cat I am.

Now look at me. Stuck in a cage. Halfway to getting a heap of horrid injections I didn't need, then lent out for all the world as if I were some rusty loft ladder, or a set of car jump leads.

Not to mention the insults. Ellie had never in all her life called me 'horribly fierce' or 'in the foulest mood'. (She called me 'spirited' instead.) She'd never lent me out, or swung me in a cage, or wrapped me up like a sausage in a fluffy pink towel. Or threatened to take me off to Spain for ever, far away from my old friends.

My friends! Dear Tiger! Fun-loving Bella! Sweet Snowball! Where would they be right now?

Mucking about, no doubt, as happily as usual on Acacia Avenue.

Having a good laugh.

Without me.

Oh, how I wished I'd never got all huffy and run away! Why had I let that grumpy Mr Glad-To-See-The-Back-Of-That-Cat drive me away? How silly of me to have allowed my-self to become jealous of that tiny fluff-ball Tinkerbell, and even that tiny human baby.

A baby! Why, the sweet little poppet had probably not been laughing at me at all. She had probably been laughing *with* me.

That is so different.

I had been so wrong! And I had nobody to blame but myself and my own foolishness. And now there was no hope of rescue. None.

17

' Haven't You Heard?'

Suddenly, through the tangles of unthreaded wool covering half the cage, I thought I saw somewhere I recognized.

Yes! Mrs Patel's grocery shop. (She *hates* me napping on her vegetables.) Arif kept walking and I thought I recognized the pizza parlour. (No need to ask. My order's pepperoni.) And then I reckoned that we must be getting near to Ellie's school because I saw the crossing guard. (Since that fur fight in the playground, she's tried to shoo me off each time we've met.)

Behind me, I heard voices. Children were gathering to cross the road, all chatting merrily.

'What's in that box you're carrying?'

'That's Harry, my stick insect. What's in your jar?'

'Bertha, my beetle.'

'I saw George bringing his rabbit.'

'Surina is bringing her mice.'

My heart leaped. Thursday! 'My Wonderful Pet Show' evening. So maybe Ellie would be walking along the street. I could yowl really loud, and maybe she would recognize my voice. I might be rescued after all!

Almost at once my hopes were dashed. The

very next thing I heard was, 'Isn't it a shame about poor Ellie?'

'Poor Ellie? Why? Isn't she coming tonight?'

'No. Haven't you heard? Her pet's been cat-napped.'

'Who, *Tuffy*? That wonderful cat she used to talk about all day?'

'Yes, that's the one.'

'So *beautiful*, she told us.'

'And *strong*.'

'And *clever*.'

'She misses him so much! She's spending all her pocket money on "lost cat" flyers, and hands them out everywhere she goes.'

'Perhaps she'll come tonight so she can give a flyer to everyone in the audience.'

'Maybe she will. But I don't think so. How could she bear to watch us all walking out of the hall so happily with our own pets? Surely she can't do that? Not even for her most beloved Tuffy!'

'Poor Ellie. Oh, poor Ellie!'

My heart sank in my boots. If Ellie couldn't bear to come, then it would be 'poor Tuffy' too!

18

All the Usual Rubbish

The children all rushed off into the school.
Then, through the tangles of woolly bits, I saw
Ellie's head teacher. She was hurrying out to
greet Arif.

'There you are! I was just getting worried.
Everyone's here, with their pets. I've even
brought my parrot Gregory to be part of the
display. And all the children are keen to listen
to your little talk about how important it is to
care for animals properly.'

Yes, I thought bitterly. Care for them *properly*.
Not swing them about in a cage.

Arif only grinned. 'Sorry,' he said. 'It took

a bit of time to lug this great big lump all the way from the park.'

Did you hear that? 'Great big lump'. Nice!

The head teacher was in too much of a hurry to bother to peer through the strands of tangled wool and take a look at me. So we went into the school hall together. Arif the Insensitive, Ellie's parrot-loving head teacher. And me.

Arif dumped my cage on the table, beside a few other pets. I took a look along the line. Pathetic! A couple of scaredy-baby mice who

cowered in their cage. (I only *looked* at them. I did *not* pretend to grab.) A bowl of brainless fish scooped out of the garden pond by that rough carrot-top gang. (The boy who'd tried to catch me was still sucking his scratches, I was glad to see.) A rabbit so old it was nearly dead. Gregory the Parrot. (At least, I guessed it was him. His cage was covered with a cloth.) A guinea pig or two. A snake. A family of hamsters. Some stupid dog that wasn't even half my size. Two whimpering gerbils.

All the usual rubbish.

Well, I consoled myself, at least I'm bound to be Star of the Show. After all, Arif was giving the talk and he'd brought *me*. He must have thought that cats were something special.

And then Arif started, lifting up each cage and bowl and box in turn along the line. He praised the fish: 'Nobody's overfed these so they're in quite splendid condition.' He cooed over the gerbils: 'Lovely cuddly things, but you must handle them gently.' Dogs: 'It is so important to train them properly.'

Bleh, bleh, bleh. On and on and on about how to care for your pets. (Try this, Arif! Don't swing them in a cage!) His talk was so, so *boring*. All that stuff you've heard a million times before about keeping the cage clean, and making sure all these pathetic pets who can't look after themselves have nice, fresh water. (Tip from myself. Save all the trouble. Get a cat!)

I could have *yowled*. But I was determined not to make a single kittenish mew in case he got annoyed and shoved me under the table, out of sight. You see, I hoped that, even though Ellie wasn't there, when Arif finally got to my

cage and pulled off the tangles of wool, someone else from Acacia Avenue would recognize
me and shout, 'Catnapper! That is Ellie's cat!
You have to give him back!'

Then I'd be rescued.

At *last* it was my turn. Arif tugged all the bits
of wool away from the wires of the cage so
everyone could see me better. And then he
held me up.

'See?' he said, shaking his head in sorrow.
'See what can happen if you aren't careful?'

I blinked. Sorry?

He kept on. 'Take this cat here. He's
obviously been brought up in a good family.
His fur is thick and glossy. His eyes are
bright. His paws are in excellent condition.'

Well, thank you, Arif. Thank you for pointing out the obvious. I am a fine, fine specimen
of a cat.

'*But*,' said Arif.

Excuse me? *But?*

I turned my head to stare. Would you
believe it? He had the nerve to carry on.

'But this pet is the *perfect* example of what

we all want to avoid in our pets. This cat has been allowed to let himself go. Recently he has been horribly, *horribly* overfed, and doesn't it show?'

He swung the cage around so that everyone could gawp at me! Cheek! I know Ms Whippy's pedal bin is a fine cornucopia of splendid grub; but surely no cat can put on that much weight in a few days . . .

Surely . . .

You wouldn't think so to listen to Arif. He was still swinging me about. 'Look at the *size* of him! Just look! No doubt this feline fellow has always teetered on the edge of getting tubby. But take a proper look. The cat inside this cage is a dire warning of what can happen if you don't keep tabs on your pet's diet. I hate to say it, but this cat is downright *fat*.'

19

Reprise

OK, OK! So put on your crossest face and shake a finger at me. I scratched him. Very hard and deep. While he was busy going on and on about how fat I'd let myself become, and how I'd get an early *heart attack* if I did not slim down to what I'd been before, I sneaked my paw through the cage bars and raked my claws right round his wrist.

That was a laugh. He yelled his head off. 'Yee-oww, yee-oww, yee-oww, yee-oww, yee-oww!'

He dropped the cage. That *hurt*. I bumped my head on the bars. So naturally I did exactly what you would have done.

Scratched him again. On the ankle.

This time he yelled even louder.

'Yee-*oww*! Yee-oww! Yee-oww! Yee-*oww*! Yee-*oww*!'

And guess what happened next. He woke up Gregory the Parrot! Don't blame *me*. How was it my fault Gregory got confused under his cover and just assumed he was at home again and we had started on a quick reprise of our wonderful *Wild Cats' Chorus*?

So Gregory started up, singing all four parts, all at once.

Loudly. *Very* loudly. So loudly that some of the more unmusical people in the hall actually put down their juice and biscuits and clapped their hands over their ears. Beside me, the hamsters started burying their heads in their bedding, trying to block out the noise. The dog was whining and drooling all at the same time. Even the snake looked rather as if it was wincing.

I thought I might as well join in and sing along. After all, it is my favourite song.

And that's when one or two of the audience

appeared to crack, grabbing their coats to rush out. (I call that very *rude*.) Gregory kept up the singing. In fact, he was now showing off, singing eight parts at once. And that's when even the people who had pets in the show began to block their ears with their fingers and rush towards the stage to snatch up their cages or boxes or fish bowl. There was a small commotion at the door because two people in the hallway were blocking everyone's path, trying to slow up the people who were hurrying out long enough to hand them a flyer.

And one of them was Ellie! Yes! Ellie! I heard her calling as the crowd forced their way past. 'Please!' she kept saying. 'Please take away with you one of these photos of my precious, lovely lost pet so you can call me if you find him.'

I didn't even crane my neck to check it was my picture that was being handed out, and not a photo of some brand-new fluff-ball kitten she'd been given called Sugar-Pie or Pansy-Wansy. I simply trusted her and saw my chance, threw back my head and yowled even louder.

'YEE-OWW, YEE-OWW, YEE-OWW, YEE-OWW, YEE-OWW. Yowwwwwl, yoWWWWL.'

Ellie knows that song! She's heard it often enough on moonlit nights.

In any case, she recognized my voice. Everyone else was running the other way, but suddenly Ellie was pushing against them, scattering flyers all over as she ran.

Straight towards me.

'Tuffy! Oh, Tuffy! I've found you at last! Thank heavens!'

I purred at her like mad.

She reached for the latch to my cage, but before she could open it, Arif stopped sucking his hand and brought it down on hers. 'Stop! Don't let this cat out. He's *vicious*.'

Ellie stared. 'He is not vicious! I should know. He's *mine*.'

Arif shook his head. 'No, no. You're wrong. Lots of cats look alike, and this one can't be yours. He is called Pusskins and he's on the way to have his shots before he goes to Spain.'

Ellie laid her hand on the cage. 'No, he is not,' she said. 'He is called Tuffy and he's had his shots already. And he belongs to me and he's so clever he was singing his favourite song just so I'd recognize him.'

'He's not yours!'

'Yes, he is. And I can *prove* it.'

Quick as a flash, she'd lifted the latch and swung the cage door open.

I'm not a cuddler, on the whole. But I wasn't going to put my pride before a rescue. I didn't muck about. I simply jumped straight into Ellie's arms and purred and purred and rubbed and rubbed, and did all those soppy and embarrassing things some hungry cats do when they don't have the guts to give you the cold blank stare that means, 'Get *on* with it, then. *Feed* me.'

'See?' Ellie said. 'Tuffy's not vicious at all. He is a wonderful, gentle, clever pet. And you can't have him.'

Arif was going to argue. But just at that moment Ellie's mother panted up behind and said, 'Yes! That is definitely our cat. And he was stolen over a week ago. We put up photos all over town. Ask anyone you like.'

Ellie squeezed me even tighter. 'See?' she told Arif. Then she slid off my fancy jewelled collar and dumped it on the table. 'But you can keep the collar and the cage.'

I owed her one, and so for once I didn't struggle. I just gave Arif the look that says, 'And you and your friend the vet can both go and boil your heads!'

Then, after Ms Whippy admitted down the phone that she had practically *kidnapped* me only a few days before, Arif *did* give up arguing, and I let Ellie and her mum take turns in carrying me home in triumph.

20

My Precious, Wonderful, Amazing Tuffy!

The moment we got near to our front door, I wriggled out of Ellie's arms. (No point in letting the child get into bad habits.)

Then, acting super-cool, I strolled back into the house. As I passed underneath a brand-new spray of glossy, waving leaves, I nodded companionably. 'Looking good, Pot Plant!'

I waved at Frying Pan and Piano – 'Hi, fellas! I'm back!' – and went upstairs, planning to say hello to Alarm Clock and Bedroom Slippers. Ellie was chasing after me, carrying my old collar. 'Oh, Tuffy! I'm so glad you're back!' She slid it over my head. It was still damp from all her weeping, but I thought I could be gracious about it. After all, the child had saved me from worse.

I let her give me the most gentle squeeze. She buried her face in my fur. 'Oh, Tuffy!' she said. 'My precious, wonderful, amazing Tuffy! The Tuffy I love so much and always have and always will, for ever and ever and ever! Thank heavens you're home and safe!'

I let her squeeze me one more time before I shook her off and went downstairs to check on Frying Pan. (After all, Ellie and her mother were both outside when that rude vet was going on about how fat I was. And I was peckish.)

21

'You Promised You'd Never Forget Me.'

Tiger and Snowball and Bella were having a laugh playing see-saw on the wobbly drain cover a few houses down.

'Hi,' I said, stepping onto Bella's side to even the game up a bit. 'It's me. I'm back.'

'Who's this?' asked Tiger.

'Do we know him?' Bella asked.

'No one I know,' said Snowball.

'Oh, come on, guys!' I told them. 'You promised you'd never forget me!'

So they knocked off the teasing and we mucked about. I told them all about my great adventures and my narrow escape. They helped me get the collar off.

'Look at the *state* of it,' said Tiger. 'Sodden! Mind you, I'm not surprised. Ellie has spent an awful lot of time these last few days howling her head off.'

'That's right,' said Snowball. 'Her mother kept on trying to cheer her up by offering her a fluff-ball kitten just like Tinkerbell.'

Tiger finished the story. 'And all she did was howl louder.'

Good stuff to hear.

We played quoits with the collar for half an hour or so while it was drying. Then the gang helped me put it on again. I think I'm safer wearing it, just for a while, until the hue and cry has all died down and Ms Whippy's found herself another mouser and flown off to Spain.

Yes. Safer here till then.

And nicer too.

At my real home. With Ellie.

PTO

The Wild Cats' Chorus

YEE-OWW, YEE-OWW, YEE-OWW,
YEE-OWW, YEE-OWW
Yowwwwwl, yoWWWWL,
Yowwwwl, yowwwl
YEE-OWW, YEE-OWW, YEE-OWW,

(*piano* – softly)

YEE-OWW, YEE-OWW, YEE-OWW,
YEE-OWW, YEE-OWW
Yowwwwwl, yoWWWWL,
Yowwwwl, yowwwl
YEE-OWW, YEE-OWW, YEE-OWW.

(*fortissimo* – very loud)

YEE-OWW, YEE-OWW, YEE-OWW,
YEE-OWW, YEE-OWW
Yowwwwwl, yoWWWWL,
Yowwwwl, yowwwl
YEE-OWW, YEE-OWW, YEE-OWW.

© Tuffy & Gang